~Three Cheers for Catherine the Great!

Throughout the text short Russian phrases follow their English equivalents to
give a sense of the difference between Catherine's language and Sara's.
The Russian letter C (as in C for Sara) is pronounced "ess."

SQUARE
FISH
An imprint of Macmillan Publishing Group, LLC

THREE CHEERS FOR CATHERINE THE GREAT!
Text copyright © 1999 by Cari Best. Pictures copyright © 1999 by Giselle Potter.
All rights reserved. Printed in China by RR Donnelley Asia Printing Solutions Ltd.,
Dongguan City, Guangdong Province. For information, address
Square Fish, 175 Fifth Avenue, New York, NY 10010.

Square Fish and the Square Fish logo are trademarks of Macmillan and
are used by Farrar Straus Giroux under license from Macmillan.

Library of Congress Cataloging-in-Publication Data
Best, Cari.
Three cheers for Catherine the Great! / by Cari Best ; illustrated by Giselle Potter.
p.   cm.
Originally published: New York: DK Pub., 1999.
Summary: Sara's Russian grandmother has requested that there be no presents at her
seventy-eighth birthday party so Sara must think of a gift from her heart.
ISBN 978-0-374-47551-2
[1. Grandmothers—Fiction. 2. Birthdays—Fiction. 3. Parties—Fiction. 4. Gifts—Fiction.
5. Russian-Americans—Fiction.] I. Potter, Giselle, ill. II. Title.
PZ7.B46575 Th 2003   [E]—dc21   2002040804

Originally published by DK Publishing, Inc., 1999.
First published by Farrar Straus Giroux
First Square Fish Edition: April 2012
Square Fish logo designed by Filomena Tuosto
mackids.com

11   13   15   17   19   20   18   16   14   12

AR: 3.2 / LEXILE: AD360L

Three Cheers for Catherine the Great!

by *Cari Best*

illustrated by Giselle Potter

SQUARE
FISH
Farrar Straus Giroux
New York

For Grandma—who started the universe—C.B.

My grandma came to America from Russia a long time
ago on a big boat with a little suitcase, three little children (Aunt Sonia,
Aunt Nina, and Anna, my mama), a little grandpa—and no English.
The man who stamped her passport couldn't say her name, Ekaterina,
so he called her Catherine. Then she had a little English, too. This is the
story of how I gave her more.

It is the dark blue of night after Mama has read me a story. Nellie the downstairs dog is snoring. He doesn't hear Mr. Minsky's cat, who has just sneaked out. Mary Caruso is singing quiet opera to Mimmo. And Mr. Minsky's toes are all tapped out.

Grandma has just had a bath with some of the leftover soap from one of her jars. "Today I am as old as all the numbers on the clock added together," she tells me.

"You'll never be too old for me," I say, getting a smile, a kiss, and a place on her lap. I love Grandma's knees and her cheeks and the sound of her Russian.

"You are my Sara forever and always," she says.

Then I notice the moon. "Look, Grandma," I say. "The moon is the letter C. C for Catherine." I write Grandma's name in English: CATHERINE.

"Tonight the moon is a Russian letter, too," Grandma says. "It is С for Sara." Grandma writes my name in Russian: Сарра.

I watch Grandma's pencil go up and down. I promise myself that I will practice writing my Russian name every single day. And maybe Grandma will teach me more.

Then Grandma and I look at each other and smile — knowing that sometimes NO PRESENTS can be the best presents of all.